Death C

Bobbie Kaald

Death Comes with the Night

Bobbie Kaald

Death Comes with the Night

By

Bobbie Kaald

Copyright @2022 by Bobbie Kaald

KDP ISBN number: 9798362796921

All rights reserved. No part of this book to be re-produced or transmitted in any form or by any means: electronic, mechanical, including photocopying, recording, or by any information storage and retrieval system; without permission in writing from the copyright owner.

This is a work of fiction. Names, characters, places, and incidents either are the product of the author's imagination or are used fictitiously, and any resemblance to any actual person, living or dead, events or locals is entirely coincidental.

Dedication

After writing the series and keeping the violence low key, I have written a prequel to the Agent Roberts/serial killer series. I need to say right up front that this book is graphic in ways the others are not.

I dedicate this book to my writers group, Writers Cooperative of the Pacific Northwest. I need to mention Toni Kief who supports me with approval but will not like this book because of the graphic nature. We all write for young adults, and this is definitely R rated.

Bobbie Kaald

Table of Content

Chapter One 11

Chapter Two 14

Chapter Three 20

Chapter Four 28

Chapter Five 32

Chapter Six 39

Chapter Seven 43

Chapter Eight 49

Chapter Nine 53

Chapter Ten 60

Chapter Eleven 64

Chapter Twelve 69

Chapter Thirteen 76

Chapter Fourteen 82

Chapter Fifteen 89

Chapter Sixteen 93

Bobbie Kaald

Chapter One

It was still dark out. There was no moon tonight at least not visible to the human eye because of the cloud layer and heavy rains. Water ran everywhere more than an inch deep. The dark figure did not worry about this because there was too much else to occupy his mind.

The figure hurried away from the doorway so recently exited, but thoughts of recent events filled every brain cell. Inside, there was carnage of a rarely seen kind. Blood splattered every surface and most of the walls up to and including some of the ceiling surface. No blood was on the shadow's clothing, and no one would think that the deed was done by the shadow. This would be the truth except that the responsibility for the deed weighed on the shadow's soul.

The weight of the guilt came from not being on time to stop the doer from any possibility of future carnage. The shadow went away to plan a way to find and stop the doer. Somehow the shadow must be faster and find the doer just at the start of the crime of carnage. The need to save the victims was the weight of the guilt the shadow carried with him as he slowly walked away. The guilt of breathing when others were not.

He hurried home without a plan to do a better job, but a better job is what he needed to do. He needed help. He knew that much. Help would find the pieces quicker. He needed to learn how to focus his mind on the important pieces from the beginning.

Opening his door on arrival, he leaned over and picked up his mail. The junk mail letters were flung at the garbage can next to the door. One important piece remained. He saw the return address was the office for the FBI training school. He couldn't remember applying for it, but this would be his answer.

Ripping open the envelope, he tore the letter inside just a little and slowed his approach. Pulling out the letter, he scanned it quickly and then reread it in disbelief. He was accepted and hadn't even applied. Who could have put his name in the hat?

"I'm going to be an FBI agent." Roberts said to himself as he put the letter in his pocket and began putting his life away as he packed and piled up the stuff to give away.

Chapter Two

It was a rugged abbreviated training period.

Roberts excelled at everything. During his interview, he mentioned his personal case and eventually the word got to the right people. His training was over, and he was assigned to a local field office in the area of his case.

Roberts was shocked and somewhat uncomfortable about bringing all his work to light with his new team. After his presentation of the facts as he knew them, his team had little to say because they were just coming on board. This was even more unnerving for Roberts.

The senior agent assigned investigations to different members and called Roberts in for a conference. Roberts slowly walked toward the office. His first day could be his last. At best, he expected to be back in school tomorrow.

When Roberts arrived in the office, he waited for his cue before moving forward. "You may shut the door and have a seat, Agent Roberts." His boss sat down and waited for Roberts to close the door and sit down.

Roberts gently closed the door because he didn't want it to accidentally slam shut. So nervous, his knees were shaking, and he nearly missed the chair when he sat down. "You wanted me?" He believed in getting right to the point and so spoke first.

"Yes, I need to have you tell me everything you know about this case and what you would do next. I know nothing about you and nothing about the case." Jarrett smiled and leaned back expecting a lengthy brief. He wasn't wrong.

Roberts nearly rolled his eyes but stopped himself and took a deep breath to relax before starting. He started at the beginning and kept going until he got to the last crime scene. "The blood was still wet, and some of it was still dripping. I left and called it in from a payphone on the corner. It amazingly still worked and wasn't torn apart."

"You did all of that on your own? Is that all in the box?" Jarrett knew the box couldn't hold much more without spilling over the side.

"Yes, I put everything in when I got assigned here. I moved into a new apartment and never had time to put it back up. There is no lunar cycle that I can see. Sometimes it's full and then at a quarter, etc." Roberts looked directly at his new boss, Jarrett, as he spoke feeling the need to establish a rapport.

"Does that mean you have no plans for further investigation?" Jarrett cut straight to the heart of the matter as he needed to get on with his day.

"I still go out after work and drive around looking for abandoned warehouses, etc." Roberts admitted.

"Good, keep me informed. In the meantime, I want you to work with Jeffries. He's retiring in a month, and I need you up to speed before that. That's all." Jarrett sat up and began leafing through his piles of papers spread around the desk.

Roberts took about three seconds before realizing he had been dismissed. He stood up and walked out of the office. He still closed the door slowly because he didn't need a reputation this early in his career. He stood there for too long and gazed at his new co-workers. Sighing, he walked back to his desk and began his day.

It was late when Roberts left the office. Just minutes ago, Susan approached him with a possible way to predict when the next murder would take place. 'It's not a lunar cycle, but the murders are a predictable number of days apart.' He thought her mad and said so. 'The first two murders were more than a year apart.'

Eventually, Susan finished her presentation and showed him that she predicted the next murder would take place in just six days. This would be thirty-nine days from the last known murder. The previous murder being forty days after the one before. The murderer was counting down, but to what end? Roberts was more than tired and called it a night after this revelation. In the morning, his brain would be reorganized after a night sleep and hopefully be able to find a place where, most likely, this next murder would occur.

As he drove home, a mantra about patterns went through his head like a song that was stuck. Patterns was what he needed to find. Patterns to places where the victims were killed and places where they were dumped or displayed. Only trouble is that not all the bodies were found, he was certain of this.

Chapter Three

Roberts slept little that night with his new mantra going through his head. He finally got up about five and took a shower and changed. He might not come home tonight depending on how it went. His coffee maker was set for four am and the coffee was still hot.

Walking out of his bedroom, Roberts grabbed the thermos and headed for the door. Putting his keys in his pocket, he reached for the doorknob when the phone rang. It was right next to the door, but he had to put the thermos down to answer it. "Hello." He didn't identify himself because no one else lived here.

"It's Susan. Can I ride with you? My car has a flat." Susan's calm voice floated out of the phone.

"I guess, but I don't know where you live." Roberts was the new kid and didn't know where anyone lived.

"I live in your building and will be standing next to your car if you agree." Susan's voice was laughing without laughter, but Roberts understood.

"You just caught me. I was just walking out and will be right down." He hung up hoping that he wasn't too abrupt.

Roberts wished he had brought another cup of coffee, but he only had two hands. The elevator ride had never seemed so long. He had made a friend, he hoped. He had few friends in life and was hoping to make some friends here at this new job. He was younger than everyone, and that might be a problem.

The door of the elevator opened, and Roberts walked out and straight ahead to his car. He could see Susan standing there holding a cup of coffee or a beverage at any rate. How had he not known that she lived here. Smiling to himself, he kept it off his face. "Get in, I just unlocked it." He said as he pushed the button in his pocket.

"Right." Susan responded automatically and got in. She found it difficult to buckle up and worry about her coffee. Spying a cup holder, she put her coffee in it while she buckled up and then retrieved the precious morning beverage.

Roberts got in as well and waited for Susan to buckle up before putting his cup in the holder and handing her the thermos. "Any thought come to you in your dreams about a site for the next murder?" He turned the car on and began backing out as he spoke.

"No. My mind is so blank that it can't even dream." Susan answered between sips of coffee.

She treasured the morning cup of coffee because the office coffee was made for Maleficent.

"I plan to spend most of the day staring at the map, like yesterday. Very productive, don't you think." Roberts was depressed to say the least and knew it was blocking his brain.

"No, I don't think so, and I plan on spending my time investigating addresses for empty facilities and then you can put a pin in the map." Susan smiled as she said this. She knew it wasn't very productive either.

"We already have red pins in the map for body dump sights. And, black pins for where the murders took place." Roberts knew where this was going but thankfully, they were in the parking lot for the office and could end this messy conversation.

"What color pin would you like for pending sites?" Susan didn't know what color they had but knew it needed to be a different color.

"White for virgin territory?" Roberts knew there was too much of a sexual connotation to that but had already said it before realizing what he said.

Susan didn't comment but changed the subject a little. "We need something to connect the murder site and the body dump site to a victim, a small number maybe." She was out of the car now and the door was shut. "Thanks for the ride." As she walked away, she made a call to a company to get her tire changed while she was at work.

They tried to stick to the plan, but they were pulled away to a kidnapping that crossed state lines. It was more than a month before they found the victim and arrested the kidnapper. The victim was very nearly dead, and the kidnapper was an uncle of the victim with a record for violent crimes.

Roberts had forgotten the deadline on his case. He was shocked back into memory by a call from his local liaison that there had been another murder just like Susan predicted.

Feeling like they had their tails between their legs. The two partners flew to the city where the crime allegedly occurred. The local FBI met them at the airport and drove them to the scene.

Roberts went in first because Susan had never been to one of the scenes in person. Pictures just can't do justice to the smell and feel of the scene. He listened to her enter and leave, as much as he expected. She returned before he completed a once over visual inspection, and then he left for some fresh air. "Let's get some air, shall we?" He didn't stop to see if she was coming.

Susan followed Roberts outside wondering why she ever asked for field work. When they passed the front door, she took a deep breath and nearly vomited again. She could still smell the pungent revolting smell of the crime scene. She would live through this but wished they had not left for their investigation of the kidnapping.

"Okay, we let the techs finish and wait for the autopsy." Roberts said. "I am going back to my map, you?" He turned and looked at his pale and somewhat green co-worker for an answer. "Perhaps, home to bed?"

That snapped her out of it. "The map if you please and my computer. We should never have been ordered to go on the kidnapping case." She stalked ahead of him to the car before her anger caused her to say something that would come around and bite her in the butt.

"I agree. I have some mints in the glovebox of my car, but we didn't come in my car." Roberts got into the backseat with Susan and nodded to the driver. He knew to take them to the office unless otherwise directed. Roberts was about ready to explode and verbally vomit on whoever or whatever was near him and kept his mouth clamped tightly shut for that reason.

"Stop at a mini-mart if you see one, thanks." Susan couldn't stop thinking of the mints now that Roberts mentioned them.

Roberts smiled at this, and his anger subsided a little. Shit happens as they say and while he knew this person didn't have to die, they would work hard on saving the rest.

Chapter Four

A week later, Roberts and Susan were making a little progress. When they returned after their new crime scene, Roberts immediately added the site and the body to the map. Why this one was left at the site of the murder would be a question that haunted him. Perhaps, a copycat.

Everything else aside, they had only thirty-eight days from the last murder. This gave them only thirty days to guess at the next sight. They began searching the empty buildings on their return to the case. They were looking for any sites of previous murders even if they were too old for a link to the victim.

To date, they only found one probable building with the same violent spray pattern of blood and pooling. They also needed to be absent of bones or corpses. It was a long shot and Roberts could only check five sites a day until he collapsed into a coma of pseudo sleep. He started on the most isolated sites and off duty officers joined in. By day twenty-nine, they had search about half of them.

Back in the office, Roberts stood in front of his inadequate board and tried to focus without much success. Susan wisely ordered out and walked over behind him with her bag of goodies. "Dinner, sir."

Roberts jumped and turned in a near pirouette. "Good thing that my gun is in my desk drawer. Dinner on you?"

Susan laughed and smiled. "I accept contributions. If you catch the guy, I will take you out to an upscale restaurant of my choice."

Roberts graciously bowed to Susan and then carried on the conversation with a smile. "Dinner would be lovely. What are we having?" He answered as he pulled out his wallet and produced a twenty. "My contribution for all your hard work."

When they finished eating, Roberts took the lead in the conversation. "Tomorrow is the day. I propose we pick which facilities to stake out."

Susan looked shocked. She lost track of where they were in the timeline. "Tomorrow?"

"Today is day thirty-seven. Let's pick the five facilities together. We are only allowed enough workforce for five." Roberts didn't look happy, and he wasn't. Getting up, he walked over to his map.

Susan was right behind him but didn't comment. "Let me pick the first one then."

"I was planning on it. The teams will be here soon for their assignments." Roberts stood back and handed her the orange pins he picked just for this stakeout.

Susan stopped for a heartbeat as she looked at the color of pin. "Appropriate. The place I pick used to be a street market." With that she poked her stick pin into the center of the old market. She also put a pin in a place not that far from the old market. "Your turn."

"You picked just the right number. I could only decide on three." Roberts put pins in his three choices and then sat down to wait for the officers who were to sit on stake out.

Susan took her cue and picked up the empty takeout containers. Then, she sat down in front of her desk to do some more research.

Chapter Five

Two days later, Roberts led the meeting of all those who were participating in this operation. He refused to think of it as a sting operation because there was never anything found. "I think we should start with anyone who had movement of any kind where they were staked out."

As he looked around the room, he saw pretty much the same look on everyone's face. No smiles were seen and no one's eyes were smiling, and no one was joking. This case was getting to everyone.

"Nothing where we were. There must have been a murder elsewhere. We need help to find the body from the site before the evidence is lost." Roberts wanted to involve the media and request help from the public, but it was not his call.

At this point, Roberts boss interrupted from the back. "It is clear that the murders will continue. I am going to hold a press conference and ask the public's help to look for blood in any of the properties that they own or have forgotten about. The banks are all making us up lists of properties foreclosed on or about to be foreclosed on. I will get those lists to Roberts as soon as I get them." He nodded then and turned to leave.

"Thanks for the assistance." Roberts didn't raise his voice but was certain that he was heard as he saw his boss nod his head. "And there we have our assignments, more research. We need to find this body before it rains. There is a hurricane season upon us and I for one want this guy in prison first. Let's get to work." He finished what he had to say and gathered up his papers that he brought just to hold. He never referred to them because his information was etched into his mind.

It was a long week of many fruitless searches, and an onslaught of phone calls on the tip line. Eventually, the body was found and a site, but the forensic team got little due to contamination by those discovering said scenes.

Roberts added the two scenes to his map and waited for the autopsy report and the miniscule forensic reports. He and Susan were back at their desks researching for the next expected heinous murder. The only had thirty-seven days from the last murder to save the next victim. No one felt hopeful that they would be able to do that.

The sun was down, and Roberts stomach was growling before he realized it. Standing up and preparing to leave, he noticed that Susan was still at her computer. "Dinner, my treat, nothing is going away, and it will still be here tomorrow."

Susan looked up at him when he spoke with glazed unfocused eyes. "What? Oh, right, dinner. I just can't quite get the answer that I need. You are right, I will try some more tomorrow, maybe it will come to me then." Shutting down her system, Susan grabbed her coat and purse as she got up and walked toward the elevator with Roberts.

"Herfy's?" Roberts jokingly asked.

"Have you lost your mind?" Susan laughed as they entered the elevator. She would have restaurant quality food if she had her way.

By the time the elevator opened to let them out, Roberts had agreed to the first restaurant that was open. He only hoped she didn't pick a place with a loud live band. He already had a pounding headache from focusing for so long.

Day twenty-nine was just as unfruitful as the previous days and for Roberts the previous months. Roberts knew he was looking for a man seething with concealed anger. He probably had a lovely, relaxed smile when he wasn't killing. The man was probably around forty and capable of locating places remote and abandoned where no one would be nosing around, and no one could hear or see what he was up to. Many of his chosen places were now known and Roberts felt that he would become anxious, maybe anxious enough to break his pattern.

As he stood analyzing his board, Roberts wondered if anyone worked up a victim's profile. He turned and saw that Susan was at her terminal. "Hey, Susan? Has anyone been able to work up a profile of the victims?"

"You know that he has no age or coloring or even racial preference. So, that would be a no." Susan didn't turn and look at him but just continued to do her research. "I will look at it again. Maybe there is something that's firmed up."

"Whose working on the missing person's files? We need to know who came back, whose body was found, who's still missing, and above all, who was killed in a similar fashion to our crimes. There are more earlier cases that have not been found, I know there are." Roberts was not talking very loudly, but Susan caught the jist of it.

"The twins are on the missing files and doing as well as we are. Sabastian is helping to create a map like yours." Susan stopped talking as some facts fell into place. "I just found another murder site. I think it is from long ago because the report says the blood was infused into the floorboards. I think that is a fancy way of saying that the blood was dried."

"I need everyone who is already working on this case in this room. Why aren't they already here? We need more desks, and everyone needs to bring their computers with them. Let's requisition this." Roberts had now passed his new shyness and moved right into being in charge. He would have made better progress if he were a seasoned agent long ago, but now was a good time for him to break out of his self-imposed restraints of timidity.

"I'll make some calls." Susan managed to keep the smile off her face as she called maintenance and all the agents she just named. She also called in an FYI call to the head of their department to update him.

Chapter Six

Two towns away, a man sat reading the news paper. It amused him to read about how close the police and FBI were to finding the killer, him. He did learn that his crimes were on a count down schedule and so, he began circling the date of his next kill on his calendar. This was convenient because it saved him a lot of work.

Amos had no respect for profilers. They thought they could read minds or some such thing. School learning had taught them nothing of importance in how other people lived and why they lived that way.

Amos knew people who were very happily living off grid and roughing it as others thought of it. Out houses were used by everyone until the invention of the toilet. Now, if you didn't have a toilet, you were crazy. He laughed at that thought. He did have a toilet, but this was a rarity.

Laying down the paper, Amos got up and went to use the toilet. Thinking about it always made him need to pee. He guessed things like that really pissed him off. Thinking that, Amos laughed at his punny.

As he went about his day, part of his mind was always thinking of the next murder. He tried to pay attention to his surroundings when others were about. He started paying better attention after someone spoke to him several times before his eyes focused enough to know who was speaking to him. It was not a pretty episode of his life.

While he was eating his dinner, Amos chose the spot for his next murder. He had chosen three sites, but he finalized in his mind an old mill site, near-by, but out of town. No one could hear the screams that inevitably came because it was too far out of town and most people would be asleep be then.

Amos saw that it was a weekday when he circled it on the calendar. People went to bed early on weeknights, even as adults. He really didn't have to worry about neighbors at the sight because the nearest 'neighbor' lives about three or four miles from the site. It was abandoned and he canvased it several time and would continue to do so in case there were any 'campers' living there.

Amos saw that it was boarded up and the surrounding area was relatively free of human leftover debris. This pleased him. He hadn't picked any particular person and would grab the first person he saw out by themselves. It was the thrill of the kill and pain that he craved. The power over another person, be they male or female, was thrilling to him. He got such a high from it that he always got an erection while he was doing it.

Amos didn't care for the clean up, and he simply left it and only took the body for confusion. He wrapped it in heavy visqueen plastic wrap and taped it shut, he heaved the body into his car and took it just anywhere. By the time he got rid of the body, he was tired beyond belief and slept for two days afterward, almost every time.

Amos only waited until he was physically recovered enough before killing again. He never knew that he was counting down until he read this in the paper. At his chosen restaurant where he ate dinner after this news was in the paper, Amos overheard someone gossiping about the police being upset that the count down was released in the paper. He nearly started laughing but paid his bill and left so he could laugh in his car.

Chapter Seven

Day thirty-six, Roberts and Susan were no where. They had no new crime scenes and no tips had paid off. The police called an hour ago and informed Roberts of a negative search on all the empty buildings. They found zero blood evidence and no evidence of an intruder.

Roberts had already decided that the perpetrator was bringing all his tools with him on the chosen day of his event. No one had ever found a murder weapon. This is just one of his pieces to confirm or deny a murder belonging to his case.

The office was more crowded now with more furniture. It looked like a newspaper or secretarial pool floor with wall-to-wall reporters working on a story. At least all the investigators were in the same office space and could talk to each other and share information and ideas.

"Okay, we need to form a plan. Hopefully with better results than the last one. We have no information with this case anymore than the other cases. We need to find this guy. I don't want him to have success again." Roberts was feeling his anger building up and getting ready to explode. He was getting better at keeping it on a tight leash but when he was younger, he had no control at all.

"I am guessing we need to have men on surveillance of all the city again. Snipers on the roof tops and the works." Emilio didn't know what else to say so he said the obvious before someone else did. Let them scramble for additional input.

"You echo my thoughts. I will let the other departments know and have them alter their patrol routes throughout the night. We have a few more days, but I believe we can use this plan on all those days. If we come up with anything else, I will share the new information with everyone." Roberts turned off his computer and sighed as he stood up. He needed a few hours sleep before the nights patrol. "I think we all should go get a few hours sleep because we have a long few days coming up." With that, he walked out of their office.

Two days later, Roberts sat in front of his computer screen with a sagging face. He knew there had been a murder somewhere. He sat by his phone because he knew someone would call eventually when they made the gruesome discovery.

When the phone rang, Roberts jumped because he must have dozed off. He looked over at the phone and it rang again. Begrudgingly, he answered it, not wanting to hear what they had to tell him. "Hello? This is Agent Roberts speaking."

Roberts listened to the report and then hung up after saying thank-you. He looked up and his co-agents were there looking at him. "They will process the evidence and send us the pictures. I wrote down the addresses if you want to go. I'm going home because I am at my end." He got up and walked out of his office looking beaten and dejected.

When Roberts was sitting in his car and reached down to start the motor, he froze, and his mind went blank. Instead of starting the car, Roberts picked up the radio microphone and called the switchboard. "This is Agent Roberts. Can I have the addresses of the crime scenes?" He scribbled them down onto his car pad and said, "out." He needed to go to the scenes even if he didn't want to.

After hanging up his mic, Roberts started the car and drove away from the federal building with the first address in mind. As he arrived, he realized this was a building he had personally searched last week. This was just crazy. Had the murderer just made this even more personal to him?

Sighing, Roberts got out and followed the line of officers into the building. "You, get this roped off and no reporters past the rope." He might as well get used to throwing his weight around as a fed.

Entering the building, he put covers on his feet but no other garb. He never touched anything. He simply made observations of his own to augment the official reports. Once he had seen them, the pictures he would be seeing were already etched into his mind.

This scene was different from the others. It was fresh. The blood pooled under the victim and ran downhill. It was an old building and the concrete floor had settled in places. Someone reached out and stopped him from advancing. The other officer pointed up. When Roberts looked, he saw blood dripping off the ceiling and then he looked at each wall only to find blood dripping down the walls in rivulets. Yes, it was fresh. They needed to stop this criminal, somehow.

"Forensics for everything. I will be at the office when I leave here, planning for his next murder. We will stop him, somehow." Roberts pronounced each word as if it were his last and an edict from hell at the same time. Turning, he stormed out of the room planning to drive around to find the dump site and be first to the body. Perhaps, he could stop him as he dumped the poor victim.

Chapter Eight

Amos sat in his car watching the murder site.

His victim was wrapped up and in the trunk. He was in the shadow of a building on the edge of this complex. Amos saw a young FBI person drive in and stop at the head of all the cars already there. The man went inside but only stayed a few moments before storming out and slamming his car door after getting inside of his car.

Amos watched the man sit in his car for a few minutes before speeding away. Once the car was nearly out of sight, Amos followed just close enough to know where this agent was. Amos didn't think the man would go to his office and he was correct. As he followed, the city faded into the background and trees jumped up in a thick grove of darkness.

Thirty minutes later, the car that Amos followed pulled off the road and Amos followed suit. He could see enough for his purpose. Amos was waiting for the man to search an area and when he left, Amos would dump the body. That way it would be days before the body would be found, if ever.

Amos waited nearly an hour. He was sorry to have had coffee for breakfast because now he needed to relieve himself, but he couldn't do that until the car drove away. As if by magic, the car owner returned and was in and driving away before Amos had his own car turned on.

Amos parked where the detective's car was parked and got out. He looked around and didn't see anyone or hear any cars or trucks coming. He quickly relieved himself before he had an accident. After doing so, he returned to the business at hand.

Amos walked to the back of his car and once again looked around and listened. He heard nothing but wanted to be quick. Dumping a body during the daylight was risky even if it was twilight. Unlocking the trunk, Amos didn't bother to focus on the interior. He leaned over and grabbed the plastic wrapped body firmly and lifted quickly. He felt his back muscles letting him know that he lifted incorrectly. He would suffer tomorrow.

Swinging the body over his left shoulder, Amos shut the trunk and walked into the underbrush and away from his car. There was a faint path through the grass that he followed. A path made by the detective who just left. The undergrowth was made up of short shrubs with thick branches and leaves that would fall soon.

Amos walked for as long as he could carry the weight of the body. When he was near collapse, he saw the path was next to a drop off and decided this was it. He turned his left side to the drop off and pushed the heavy weight off his shoulder. Feeling immediate relief, Amos watched as the body rolled out of sight and down into oblivion. The brush popped back into place to obscure any look of recent passage.

Amos smiled as he walked back to the car. This was his best drop spot yet. It would be months, if ever, before the body was discovered. The leaves would fall, but the snow might come first and cover the body. By the time the snow melted, and the air warmed up enough to tempt hikers out, the leaves would be back. No one would ever find his hidden evidence.

Chapter Nine

Susan couldn't sleep that night. Her own personal guilt made her mind churn and inflamed her thoughts. She heated up the leftover coffee and headed into the office to try to make a new course for their investigation. She was tired though and nearly as soon as she sat down at her desk, Susan fell deeply asleep. This is how Roberts found her when he came in roughly at his regular start time.

Roberts saw Susan asleep at her desk and surmised what happened. He decided to allow her what peace she could have for this small moment and went about his own morning of rechanneling his enemy. He searched for hours after work and found nothing.

In bed last night and this morning, Roberts slept fitfully and had broken dreams. Dreams that led his mind around to an inescapable conclusion. This killer was playing with them. Susan's idea was sound as far as it went but the killer read it in the paper or something. Roberts woke up certain that the killer would change his MO.

"When did you get in?" Susan spoke from behind him in a crackly voice of just awakening and then coughed to clear her voice.

"How long did you work last night and why don't you sleep at home?" Roberts smiled as he turned back.

"I can't answer that. But I can tell you that my mind wouldn't shut up last night." Susan laughed too and got up to go find the restroom. "I'll be right back." With that she was gone, and Roberts was alone with his board.

Roberts sipped his coffee and stared at his board. His eyes were ever moving as his brain double checked his previous conclusions. He could hear the others entering behind him. "Any news?" There wouldn't be any, yet.

"The evidence summary is here. As we all knew, it is short sweet and to the point. There is nothing pertinent." Sebastian spoke as he handed over the faxed report and then returned to his desk.

"That was expected." Roberts took the time to look it over and then looked up at his team. "There is some indication of a male person that wasn't associated with the blood. It is probably some vagrant who was just passing through in the last week or so. Even so, make a copy of this and I will put it on the board." Roberts was beginning to form a new plan.

The work was tedious and boring and mesmerizing, but still they had no suspects. The entire team worked long hours to try to tie up all the loose ends. The time was slipping by without a conclusion.

It was at the halfway mark to their endpoint deadline, a Massachusetts Patrolman came to their building and asked to see the team. Of course, everyone wanted him to come up because he must have some information for them. Roberts walked over and opened the door to their room and watched the elevator door for his arrival.

The door opened and a middle-aged police officer walked out of the elevator carrying two full boxes of papers. He turned and saw Agent Roberts standing in the doorway waiting for him. "Roberts, you're expecting me?" He spoke as he walked and walked past Roberts without stopping. "If you don't mind these are heavy."

Roberts was unable to grab one to assist him because the police officer was almost to the table where he put the boxes down. Turning around,

Agent Roberts introduced himself. "I am Agent Roberts. How can I help you?" He knew it was the wrong wording but couldn't stop himself.

"It is what I hope that I can do for you. I am the major crimes officer for my station. I have accumulated all these cases and don't know if they can help you. They were all gruesome in the extreme. The bodies that we found were found elsewhere." The man stopped talking for a minute and then started again. "I'm sorry. I can be so rude, let me introduce myself. I am Officer Cjse of the Patrol."

"This is Susan, Sebastian, Fred, and Walter. How many cases are we talking?" Agent Roberts was nearly salivating as he looked at the boxes.

Cjse took his cue and continued. Reaching over to open the top box, he answered. "Twenty or thirty." The silence of the room said it all. He continued, "I hope you already know about most of them."

"Okay then, let me read off the names and Susan can tell us if it's new to us. Are any of these from outside of Maryland?" Roberts tried not to feel overly frustrated, but he was feeling that.

For the next hour, the team compared the names on the files to the ones they already knew about. There were few duplicates which increased Roberts depression and feelings of uselessness.

When they had finished, the Officer cleared his throat a few times and clearly had something to say. Finally, he sighed and spat it out. "The boss told me to ask if you wanted a liaison person and volunteered me because I already have information. Information in these files." Csje looked down at his shoes because no FBI person ever wanted help.

Roberts looked shocked. "You would be on duty but working here? Your hours being billed to your own unit?"

"I'm not certain how they do it, but I wasn't told any different." Csje nodded as he spoke.

"Let me make a call." Roberts picked up the phone on his desk and dialed his boss. He relayed the information and listened. Mouthing that he was on terminal hold.   The others got back to sorting the files.

After about fifteen minutes of uselessness, Roberts hung up and announced to the room. "I want everyone to welcome Csje to the team." No one did more than nod and continued working.

Chapter Ten

Amos woke up days later mostly because his stomach was growling and somewhat crampy. He couldn't remember taking a shower when he got back so he took off all his clothing and threw it down the laundry chute. He took a long shower soaping everything and everywhere with his chosen soap. Afterward he used scented men's cologne and checked his non-existent beard. He still didn't need to shave.

He went downstairs in the buff and put his clothing in a double wash double rinse with borax and borateem. This would get out any blood residue and leave a warm soft scent that women liked. When he saw a woman looking at him, his heart would skip a beat as his brain remembered past adventures. Women looked at him when he smelled loving, and he loved it.

Amos left the washer to do it's thing and went to the kitchen for something to eat. As he sat eating what he quickly prepared, Amos mentally thought of everything he needed to do and soon. He usually lucked out with the monetary means found on his victim. He moved too soon and took only a vagrant as it turned out. The man had less funds than Amos, but Amos rent was due.

"Well, it was fun to play the count down game, but it is over." Amos spoke to the air and got up to prepare for the day.

Amos left his dishes in the sink and would do them after he had his last meal of the day. He left the house through the garage and locked the door behind himself. No sense in coming home to someone like himself inside of his safety area. Shutting the door behind himself, he twisted the lever to assure himself that it was locked, and it was.

Amos walked over and got into his car. He would drive to a building that he knew from his last canvas of empty buildings. The traffic was heavy and slow this time of the day and this allowed him time to visualize the surrounding area for police surveillance. He knew they were watching the buildings and he was very careful. If all went well, he would move on after this one. He got restless when he stayed more than a couple of months in one area.

Amos was satisfied that no one was watching this building. There weren't even any street people hanging around pretending to belong. He drove home and parked his car. He would wait until late and then nab a likely person to make them disappear into the chosen building. Entering his current flop house, Amos locked himself in and went over to the couch. He was asleep almost before his head touched the armrest.

Chapter Eleven

Roberts fell asleep in his car as he sat watching for movement. They worked late together and ended up with nearly twice as many cases as they had before the new boxes arrived from the Maryland Patrol. Each person chose a building and left separately with handheld radios in hand. He had a sinking feeling in his chest that he could not place or shake. This nemesis was not that predictable in his opinion, yet Susan had predicted his last kill. Was she right?

Roberts didn't want to risk that she was wrong and asked for surveillance for this month. His boss eventually called him with approval, or he would be here without pay because he was going to do this anyway. About half of the other buildings were being surveilled by other committed officers from various police forces.

Roberts dozed off before the sun came up and was awakened by a flashlight clanging against his window. Jolted awake, he sat up and looked around. Seeing an officer at his window, he rolled the glass down. "Sorry, officer, I fell asleep."

"No one in your building, I checked the whole thing myself just now." The officer spoke to Roberts and turned to continue his patrol.

"Thanks for letting me know." Roberts answered as the officer walked away. He didn't know it was Amos, the very murderer that he was seeking. He would know very soon because he got out and began his morning search for signs of anyone being in the building.

Slowly, Roberts walked forward around abandoned furniture and boxes. Nothing seemed out of place and unexpected. A few feet inside though, he saw a footprint in the dust and walked the way the footprint led him. Here and there he saw another footprint and as he rounded a corner, in front of him was the blood bath.

Realizing his mistake, Roberts turned and ran out of the building to try to find the officer. Of course, the officer was gone or who ever he was. He must have been the killer.

Roberts went to his car and called for a forensic team. He planned to have his drivers door fingerprinted in case there was anything from the man waking him up. As he waited for the crime people his anger began to increase and his thoughts became clearer. This was now personal between the killer and him. He accepted that and would try to outthink him. Clearly, he was not on a timetable anymore if he ever was.

The forensic team came and found only smudges. Even his own fingerprints were obliterated. Roberts decided the person doing this was wearing gloves. He had known that all along and now they would wait for blood typing to come back. He longed for improved tests, but he would have to wait, patience not being his long suit.

Hours later, Roberts was released to return to the office. All documentation was completed on site and as much evidence of their presence as possible was removed. Lastly, and only for aesthetics, several blowers were brought in and the dust from the floor was blowen around so much that most of it was in the air. The technicians backed out and hoped to not have left many shoe impressions behind.

The sun was going down as Roberts headed to the office. He was nearly there when he decided enough was enough and called to say that he was falling asleep at the wheel and would not be in until he got some sleep. With that, Roberts drove home and fell into bed as soon as he reached it.

He was in such oblivion that the multiple phone calls did not wake him up.

Chapter Twelve

Sandra was not too tired to work. She had not been on a voluntary stakeout last night and didn't know Roberts was on one. That is until he didn't show for work and all the forensic personnel suddenly disappeared for hours. She thought Roberts would come in eventually, but he didn't.

By the time Sandra went home for the day, she learned that the killer had struck again last night. She knew there would be harassment of a jovial nature tomorrow, and for days to come, having to do with the count down schedule that he was obviously not using anymore.

Roberts awakened at a very early hour and was unable to return to sleep. He got up eventually and showered before getting dressed for the day. His coffee maker clicked on while he was showering, and he grabbed a to go mug of coffee and filled his thermos.

Smiling, Roberts left his apartment and walked to the elevator. It arrived quickly because of the early hour, and he entered. Pushing the L button on his way in, Roberts nearly spilled his coffee as the elevator quickly began to descend. "Shit," quietly slipped out of his mouth but before the door opened.

When the door opened, he walked slowly over to his car stopping now and again to take a sip of the cooling coffee. He could feel his brain cells opening up slowly. He very nearly decided to take everything off the board and start again. Nothing they were doing was helping and a new approach might be needed.

Snug in his car, and his coffee safely in the cup holder, Roberts began his commute to work. He blew nearly a day and would have to make up for it.

As Roberts walked into the office he stopped in his tracks. The board was completely different. Someone had been very busy. "Well, I guess someone doesn't need me anymore." Walking forward as he spoke, he unloaded on his desk. Turning around he looked at the board. "So, fill me in."

Susan startled but only for a second. Smiling she began to fill Roberts in. "There were so many new victims that we took everyone down and slowly put them in order of disappearance. I thought the oldest date in each file would help us narrow things down."

"You have done a splendid job. You know he is no longer, if ever, adhering to a count down cycle." Roberts announce his most recent conclusion.

"At least not now. The papers broke that and now he will change up." Susan admitted reluctantly. She leaked it to the papers and now she knew the consequences.

"We will have to trip over him while he is in the act to catch him, now." Roberts spoke softly but Susan heard. She didn't comment.

Finally, Susan spoke her piece. "A bit negative, but accurate."

Robert stood looking at the rearranged display. "I like the order and under each picture is where the body was found, if it was." He had to walk side to side to take in all the pictures. Some were sketches as no picture could be found and the identity of the victim remained obscure.

"I am glad that you approve. It is your area, and I was worried about how you would feel." Susan got up and walked over next to him. "The board on the left has a map on it. I put red pins in all the buildings found to be murder sites."

Roberts interrupted Susan, "and I see blue pins were there are empty buildings. What's this orange pin?"

"That is where he almost killed you, silly." Susan smiled and continued. "I made it orange as a kill site without a body, but it may not be the same person."

"Good thinking, but it is the same guy. It's just not in your pattern." Roberts sat down in his office chair and leaned back to get a better view without killing his neck quite so much. "So, we need daily reconnaissance of the empty buildings. A grueling task and I can't imagine how we will accomplish this."

"Good luck getting approval for stakeouts." Susan returned to her desk. "I still have a few of the patrol files to go through. She looked up at

Roberts as she spoke and gasped. "Come over here and look at the map. I think I am losing my mind."

Roberts kept quiet because he didn't want to interrupt her thinking process. Instead, he obliged her and walked over behind her and looked at the map. "Okay, I am looking. What are you seeing?"

"Look at all the pins and let your mind solve the picture puzzle." Susan offered without conviction that he would be able to do it. "I see a circle with piece cut out of it." She got up and went over to the map pointing as she revolved around the pattern that she thought was forming.

"Only one spoke missing." Robert walked up next to her. "This is the building we need to watch." He stabbed his thumb at the existing blue pin so hard that he nearly punched a hole in his fingertip. Pulling his hand away reflexively. "Agreed?"

"Absolutely." Susan grabbed her things. "I need some sleep. You are caught up. Pick me up at the garage when you are heading to the building." With that, she flew out of the office and to her apartment.

Chapter Thirteen

Amos slept around the clock after getting home. When he woke up, he showered and went out to find some food at a diner or somewhere with people and a paper. When he found a table with a leftover paper on it, he was elated. This didn't last because he found nothing written on his latest murder.

Amos clenched his teeth closed to prevent accidental exclamations of pure hate. He paid for his food and left taking the paper with him. He planned to move again tomorrow. Today he walked slowly around his chosen building but saw nothing. Nothing moved and no one was around. This was a little rare, but not unheard of. His need to fulfill this last building and get out of town blocked everything else out of his mind.

All light was gone now from the sky and the streets. Amos sprinted across the street and behind trucks or anything else in the parking lot to stay hidden from any potential passers by. It took about half an hour before he found an unlocked door and entered his building.

The door banged shut behind him and Amos jumped. He should have been more careful. Walking forward, Amos covered his face as the dust swirled up about him from his passing. This was the worst building he could have chosen. Further away from the door, the dust seemed to be less and settled down closer to the floor. As he rounded a corner, he saw another room and walked over to see what he could use.

As he investigated the room, he saw a large desk that would do nicely for his table. The rest he would bring with him tonight. Smiling, he turned and followed his footsteps out of the building. He propped the outside door open to let any wind in and blow the dust around to cover most of his passing.

He glanced around as he returned to his car and saw nothing that seemed to have changed from when he entered. Tonight, would work, and then he would leave town as he disposed of the body. Maybe, he should just leave it. He couldn't decide, but time would tell. He had been known to change his mind.

As Amos drove away from his building, he decided that the time had come. It was as dark as the city ever became. Time to cruise around, hit the beach, walk the city if he had to. He would try the beach first. He nearly forgot that the beaches closed at dark, but did everyone adhere to that?

It took a while to reach the beach, but he didn't drive past anyone walking the streets out alone. Parking as close to the gate as he was able to, Amos got out and began walking toward the beach.

Walking quietly and staying to the shadows, Amos watched for anyone else walking around or sitting and watching the waves. He walked through the empty parking lot and listened for the noise of another person. It was tricky, but there was always someone not caring about the rules. Someone who had a fight and was walking off their anger, or someone down on their luck would be his luck and the end of theirs.

The tide was out now for the night but would come in again before morning. Amos stayed above the tide mark. The large driftwood trees lay along the mark and were excessively dry and white as bones, thus the term, dry as bones. Eventually, Amos picked a log to sit on and await his new friend who would come soon.

There was a gentle breeze when Amos first arrived, but it was picking up now and if it got much worse Amos would have to leave and try somewhere else. Finally, Amos tired of the wind and got up to leave. As he walked back to his car, a man approached him. 'Great, a park ranger rick.' Amos muttered to himself as he braced for a lecture.

But it wasn't a ranger, it was a homeless man scamming for a freebie. "Do you have a camp down here?" The man asked trying not to shiver from insufficient clothing for the weather.

"No, I was just watching the waves. I'm on my way to my car. I just got groceries and they are still in the trunk. Come along and I will give you something to eat." Amos answered with his most convincing tone of voice.

"That would be great." The man answered and walked beside Amos because he didn't know where Amos car was. "I don't suppose you have a coat?"

"I just might have something." Amos answered and nearly gave him his coat because it was short term but didn't want to risk a bug infestation.

The two men walked on in silence with Amos slightly ahead of the homeless man, but never taking his ears off of the man's movements. Amos pushed a button in his pocket and the trunk opened as they approached.

This caused an unconscious action on the other man's part as he rushed to see what there was. As he passed Amos, something hit him in the head, and he blacked out slumping into the open trunk.

It took little practiced effort on Amos part and the man was inside the trunk with the lid closed. There was nothing else in the trunk.

Amos looked around as he walked to the drivers door and let himself inside. Everything was going as he planned it. Everything that he knew about. He started the car and began driving out of the park area and took the long way to the abandoned building ever watching for the police of any sort.

Chapter Fourteen

Minutes after deciding on the building, Roberts and Susan got on the phone and orchestrated a stake out of the building, warehouse as it turned out, from all sides. Roberts would take the front. His partner would come with him. The two new boys wanted the back and that left the sides for SWAT and the city boys.

Roberts opened his desk and took his two pairs of binoculars, and his night vision goggles. He looked up and Susan had her latest telescopic camcorder. She came back in because she couldn't sleep. They walked out together and stopped by the armory and signed out a sniper rifle with a night vision super powerful scope. They were set. He had a stakeout bag of munchies in the trunk, and they were soon on their way to a building across the street from the gate to this warehouse.

"I am going to park in the back and enter the back door. Our room is in the front. The owner said we could have it for free if we mention his name in the news cast after the capture." Roberts spoke to the air and really didn't think Susan would answer.

"Greedy bastard." Susan said with disgust. "I hate media, but I hate media mongers more."

Roberts glanced over at Susan because he had never heard her speak so. Everyone that he knew would have to agree with her, but Roberts found them an easy way to leak select information as a way of advancing the case. He was busy driving and didn't comment.

Parking his car in the shadows, he whispered to Susan before getting out. "Shut and lock the door silently. All we need is for this murderer to steal my car as a way of making his escape." With that, Roberts got out and took his equipment with him, slowly closing the door a final tap with his arm closed his door with a soft click. Smiling, he looked around for a door.

Seeing the door that the building owner told him to use, he walked up to it and opened it for Susan and himself to enter. Just then, Roberts remembered he would need a walkie-talkie. "I don't suppose you brought a walkie with you?"

"Actually, I have one in the bag, and I just hope the batteries last." Susan's voice came from behind him as they walked upstairs to their chosen room with a view of the warehouse.

Amos had been driving through the city for some hours now. He was certain that he was not being followed but he was just letting his car go where it wanted to. Soon, he would park at the warehouse and the evening's festivities could commence.

Amos was smiling in anticipation and took the next corner. One more corner and he would arrive. At the next corner, Amos looked around in all directions save up. Feeling clear of authorities, he turned in and drove up next to the building in the shadows. As he got out, he could not hear any movement. Good, he could start right away.

Amos opened the door and left it open. The inside lights were disabled. Taking the keys with him, he walked quickly to the trunk carrying the crowbar from beside the drivers seat, always a ready tool for temporarily making someone unconscious.

Opening the trunk, Amos was prepared but saw no sign of consciousness even when he poked his victim with the crowbar. Sliding the crowbar into his belt, Amos lifted the package and slung it over his shoulder. He closed the lid as softly as he could with full hands and proceeded inside of the warehouse. Cursing softly under his breath for not propping the door open, Amos was soon inside.

Roberts saw a man getting something heavy out of his trunk and enter the building. "Susan call everyone to come to this building, now."

Susan did so and they waited as long as their nerves would allow before leaving their post and taking their weapons with them to head for the building to confront the killer and hopefully save the victim.

As they were leaving the building cars started pulling up and stopping to block the gate. They entered together and walked directly to the door behind the car. They entered one at a time in a silent mode. From there they took separate vectors until the killing site was found.

When the discovery was made, the victim was tied to a table and the perpetrator was approaching with a knife held high. He was muttering unintelligible sounds, but the first man on the scene didn't wait to ask what he said. The officer yelled police and shot him twice until he fell down and no longer moved.

Roberts came right behind him. "Is he dead? We can't ask him anything." Walking forward, Roberts checked, and the perpetrator was dead. Turning to the victim, he and Susan spoke to him as they untied him. "We are the FBI, and the man is dead. We will have you checked out and return you to your home." He knew it would not actually happen quickly and smoothly, but it was reassuring to the victim to hear this. He supposed he would now return to finish the training and he wanted that.

"Your first capture?" An officer walked up behind him to congratulate him.

Roberts got his wish and returned to training. He didn't feel confident with being in charge yet. Susan took over and remained at her desk until he returned two years later.

Chapter Fifteen

Finally, Roberts received his certificate and a commission to return to the department for capturing serious serial killers. Susan was outside to meet him and take him where he wanted to go. Eventually, she would tell him why she was really here.

Roberts could read her like a book even before this last two years. "Hello, Susan. Why are you really here?" He just wanted to get to the heart of the matter. He needed a couple of weeks off to rest his brain.

Susan faked looking shocked. "Roberts, I came to pick you up and take you back to your desk that I have saved for you because we all knew you would be back where you belong."

"I have a car, and things to pack." Roberts had become professional at stating the obvious.

"Okay. I can't fool you. We are needed in Minnesota." There she said it and she hadn't even congratulated him on his graduation from the FBI academy.

"Okay then. As it happens, I already packed, and my stuff is all in my car. I just need to ditch it in a safe place, and we will be off to your first cases with a Newby partner." Roberts walked away from Susan, but she followed along.

"Hardly a Newby." Susan said in matter-of-fact tone of voice.

"Officially, a Newby." Roberts said as he walked beside her. "My car awaits your command." A good time to joke before things get disgusting, always Roberts thought.

"I will leave my car here for now, and ride along." Susan said as she tried to get in. "Door's locked." Looking Roberts in the eye as she said this and remembering his humor and why she had missed him.

"I will let you in when you tell me where we are going." Roberts got in but left her door locked just for a second.

"You are so not funny. Drive to the local airport, as in the closest one. We have a plane waiting to take us to Minnesota." Susan said as she got into the car once the door was finally unlocked.

The trip to Minnesota was a waste because the perp was located, before they landed. The did a cursory walk through the scene and left it in the hands of the locals. Roberts was proud of Susan who held her cookies through it all.

When they returned to the plane, Roberts heard Susan throwing up in the restroom. He felt like doing the same and said nothing upon her taking her seat next to him. "You going to be okay?"

"I don't want to talk about it, ever." Susan said with her eyes closed and head leaned back.

"Mint?" Roberts somehow always had a pack of tic-tacs with him and he held it out to Susan.

Susan took the proffered mints even as she glared at Roberts. After downing a handful, she handed them back. "Thanks."

"Don't mention it. I will drop you off and meet you at the office. I need to arrange for housing for tonight." Roberts said and leaned up against the window to let his stomach settle. He thought the bloody scenes were bad, but cannibalism topped it big time.

Chapter Sixteen

The years that followed were a blur for Roberts. Each case was unique, but the murderers were complex. Eventually, the FBI had Roberts touring the country talking about the cases and helping other agents be more effective.

It was ego inflating and interesting, but emotionally exhausting. Roberts slept for a full day on returning from each case. During the cases he became obsessed and slept little, thus sleeping when he returned.

There was a certain amount of monotony with the serial killer cases, for that is all they assigned him because he had experience and brought in the killer. Roberts started by feeling emotional pain and empathizing with the victims. After a while, he became encased in a shell of disinterest and a certain number of unfeeling attitudes descended on him.

Eventually, Susan resigned and moved on because she didn't want what happened to Roberts to happen to her. She had a family and young children that needed her to be human and not a robot. She used this as her reason to leave. Her resignation was accepted as inevitable because eventually everyone resigned. Hopefully, they resigned before becoming broken.

When Roberts was on the edge of mandatory retirement, they got a call from Western Washington about tons of missing persons. The real pressing issue was a child's skeleton being found buried within the town limits of a small town east of Everett. He agreed to go on the grounds that this would be his last case.

Years later, Roberts remembered this conversation verbatim. He laughed every time he remembered it because it was years before he brought it to a close.

Bobbie Kaald

Death Comes with the Night

Bobbie Kaald

Made in the USA
Middletown, DE
20 November 2022